Samuel French Acting Edition

Off Off Broadway Festival Plays 45th Series

Slow Jam
by Caity-Shea Violette

The Falling Man
by Gethsemane Herron

Voir Dire
by Carissa Atallah

I Didn't Think You'd Be So Unhappy
by Shara Feit

Masking Our Blackness
by Vincent Terrell Durham

Crush
by Krista Knight

ISBN 978-0-573-70914-2

www.concordtheatricals.com
www.concordtheatricals.co.uk

FOR PRODUCTION INQUIRIES

UNITED STATES AND CANADA
info@concordtheatricals.com
1-866-979-0447

UNITED KINGDOM AND EUROPE
licensing@concordtheatricals.co.uk
020-7054-7200

Each title is subject to availability from Concord Theatricals Corp., depending upon country of performance. Please be aware that *OFF OFF BROADWAY FESTIVAL PLAYS, 45TH SERIES* may not be licensed by Concord Theatricals Corp. in your territory. Professional and amateur producers should contact the nearest Concord Theatricals Corp. office or licensing partner to verify availability.

starting rehearsals, advertising, or booking a theatre. A licensing fee must be paid whether the title(s) is presented for charity or gain and whether or not admission is charged. Professional/Stock licensing fees are quoted upon application to Concord Theatricals Corp.

This work is published by Samuel French, an imprint of Concord Theatricals Corp.

No one shall make any changes in this title(s) for the purpose of production. No part of this book may be reproduced, stored in a retrieval system, scanned, uploaded, or transmitted in any form, by any means, now known or yet to be invented, including mechanical, electronic, digital, photocopying, recording, videotaping, or otherwise, without the prior written permission of the publisher. No one shall share this title(s), or any part of this title(s), through any social media or file hosting websites.

For all inquiries regarding motion picture, television, online/digital and other media rights, please contact Concord Theatricals Corp.

MUSIC AND THIRD-PARTY MATERIALS USE NOTE

Licensees are solely responsible for obtaining formal written permission from copyright owners to use copyrighted music and/or other copyrighted third-party materials (e.g., artworks, logos) in the performance of this play and are strongly cautioned to do so. If no such permission is obtained by the licensee, then the licensee must use only original music and materials that the licensee owns and controls. Licensees are solely responsible and liable for clearances of all third-party copyrighted materials, including without limitation music, and shall indemnify the copyright owners of the play(s) and their licensing agent, Concord Theatricals Corp., against any costs, expenses, losses and liabilities arising from the use of such copyrighted third-party materials by licensees. For music, please contact the appropriate music licensing authority in your territory for the rights to any incidental music.

IMPORTANT BILLING AND CREDIT REQUIREMENTS

If you have obtained performance rights to this title, please refer to your licensing agreement for important billing and credit requirements.

Concord Theatricals presents The Samuel French Off Off Broadway Short Play Festival (OOB) has been the nation's leading short play festival for forty-five years. The OOB Festival has served as a doorway to future success for aspiring writers. Over 200 plays have been published, and many participants have become established, award-winning playwrights.

For more information on the Off Off Broadway Short Play Festival, including history, interviews, and more, please visit www.oobfestival.com.

Festival Sponsor: Concord Theatricals

Festival Artistic Director: Casey McLain
Literary Manager: Garrett Anderson
Client Manager: Abbie Van Nostrand
Festival Moderator: Amy Rose Marsh
Marketing Team: Jeremiah Hernandez, Courtney Kochuba,
Annette Storckman, Imogen Lloyd Webber
Festival Staff/Readers: Tyler Mullen, Rosemary Bucher, Sarah Weber,
Alex Perez, Fiona Kyle, Rachel Levens, Elizabeth Minski,
Charlie Coulthard, Rachel Smith, Maria Arroja Ferriera, Meg Schadl,
Skylar Wilkins, Debbie McLean, Jeremiah Hernandez, Teresa Castro,
Zach Kaufer, Scott Stait

HONORARY GUEST PLAYWRIGHT
Dominique Morisseau

FESTIVAL JUDGES
Larissa FastHorse
Nan Barnett
Will Arbery
Karen Zacarias
Kimber Lee
Susi Westfall
Nambi E. Kelley
Madhuri Shekar
George Brant

TABLE OF CONTENTS

FOREWORD

Concord Theatricals is honored to have the six daring and inspirational playwrights included in this collection as the winners of our 45th Annual Off Off Broadway Short Play Festival. This year our Festival received over 500 submissions from around the world. We thank all of these gifted playwrights for sharing their talent with us and welcome each writer into our elite group of Off Off Broadway Festival winners.

When we sat down to plan our 45th consecutive year of the OOB Festival, our team recognized that some changes would have to take place due to COVID-19. However, we found it reassuring to reflect on our past festivals, which have ranged in evaluation format and performance presentation.

This year, to ensure the safety and wellbeing of everyone involved, we removed the performance aspect and went back to our roots by choosing the six winners through reading evaluation only. We missed our extended OOB Festival theatre family – the actors, directors, stage managers, and tech crews – but we were excited to focus directly upon that which the festival was built: the script and the playwright.

From our initial pool of Top-Thirty playwrights, we ultimately select six plays for publication and representation by Concord Theatricals. Of course, we can't make our selections alone, so we enlist some brilliant minds within the theatre industry to help us in this process. We invited an esteemed group of nine judges consisting of a mix of Concord Theatricals playwrights and members of the theatre industry. We thank them for their support, insight, and commitment to the art of playwriting.

Concord Theatricals is the world's most significant theatrical company, comprising the catalogs of R&H Theatricals, Samuel French, Tams-Witmark, and The Andrew Lloyd Webber Collection. We are constantly striving to develop groundbreaking methods that will better connect playwright and producer. With a team committed to continuing our tradition of publishing and licensing the best new theatrical works, we are boldly embracing our role in this industry as bridge between playwright and theatre.

On behalf of the entire Concord Theatricals team in our New York, London, and Berlin offices, and the over 10,000 playwrights, composers, and lyricists that we publish and represent, we present you with the six winning plays of the 45th Annual Samuel French Off Off Broadway Short Play Festival.

This festival is about playwrights. Sharing the human story. We invite you to enjoy these extraordinary plays.

Casey McLain
Artistic Director
The Samuel French Off Off Broadway Short Play Festival

Slow Jam

Caity-Shea Violette

SLOW JAM was developed through a series of virtual workshops with the John F. Kennedy Center for the Performing Arts in July 2020.

SLOW JAM was virtually produced by the Kennedy Center American College Theater Festival as the winner of the 2020 Gary Garrison Ten-Minute Play Award on September 11, 2020. The director and sound designer was Jeremiah Davison. The cast was as follows:

JAMIE... Garret Turner
CHARLIE... Jerrie Johnson
STAGE DIRECTIONS................................... India Tyree

CHARACTERS

JAMIE – Mid-to-late twenties, any gender, any ethnicity. Finds comfort in control. Really trying.

CHARLIE – Mid-to-late twenties, any gender, any ethnicity. Not sure how to do this. Also really trying.

SETTING

The bedroom of a small apartment in a city – their first place together

TIME

Present day

AUTHOR'S NOTE

Pronouns can be adjusted to match each performer's gender identity.

(Jamie and Charlie's bedroom, late evening.)

*(**CHARLIE** sits on the bed. They sip mid-shelf whiskey from a rocks glass probably purchased at T.J. Maxx. There is another glass on the nightstand.)*

*(**CHARLIE** lights a candle and is immediately unsure where to put it. They try at least two places.)*

(A knock on the door.)

CHARLIE. *(Casual sexy voice.)* Come in...

*(**JAMIE** carefully opens the door, trying to enter without letting the cats in. They are wearing something sexy and revealing, also probably from T.J. Maxx.)*

JAMIE. Did anybody get in?

CHARLIE. I think you made it.

(A breath. They look at each other.)

Hey sexy.

JAMIE. Hey.

*(**JAMIE** hands **CHARLIE** a drink. They clink glasses and sit beside each other in bed.)*

JAMIE.	**CHARLIE.**
Should we set the timer? I think we set the timer first.	So do we just start or – Right – the timer.

*(**JAMIE** grabs their phone to set the timer.)*

JAMIE. Maybe you could find us some music?

CHARLIE. Oh, uh – sure.

JAMIE. I thought it might be fun to – I don't know it might be dumb.

CHARLIE. What were you thinking?

JAMIE. I don't know, is there like a standard sort of –

CHARLIE. Like a *Slow Jam*?

JAMIE. Yeah but like for anxious people from the Midwest.

CHARLIE. On it.

> (**CHARLIE** *searches on their phone.*)

JAMIE. Also probably something with no lyrics or else I'll just be thinking about the lyrics...

CHARLIE. Assuming no jazz?

JAMIE. Jazz is fine.

CHARLIE. You hate jazz.

JAMIE. I don't *hate* jazz, I just find brass instruments abrasive and I prefer musicians to prepare their work ahead of time.

CHARLIE. Yeah you definitely hate jazz.

> (*Beat.*)

JAMIE. I'm trying to be open to new things, okay?

CHARLIE. Sorry, I wasn't trying to shut you down.

JAMIE. It's fine.

CHARLIE. Let's do jazz.

JAMIE. It's gonna feel weird now.

CHARLIE. If it feels weird, we'll turn it off. You set the timer, I'll find the music.

(They do.)

JAMIE. Okay ready when / you are –

CHARLIE. Just scrolling through options quick...

*(They sit in silence while **CHARLIE** scrolls.)*

JAMIE. ...How's it going over there?

CHARLIE. Sorry I'm getting weird results.

JAMIE. What did you search?

CHARLIE. *(Earnestly.)* "Sexy-jazz-no-lyrics-minimal-brass."

JAMIE. Maybe lose the last half of that.

CHARLIE. Okay – okaaaay. There's something called "Rain and Jazz"?

JAMIE. Go on...

CHARLIE. The description says "relaxing rainstorm with lyricless smooth jazz for coffee shops, study sessions, or romantic evenings." Does that not feel like three very different moods?

JAMIE. It's fine – let's just try it.

CHARLIE. You sure?

*(**JAMIE** kisses **CHARLIE**'s shoulder.)*

Rain and Jazz it is.

*(**CHARLIE** presses play, and they begin slowly, tenderly touching. An advertisement abruptly blares from the phone.)*

ADVERTISEMENT. SWITCH NOW TO SPRINT / WIRELESS AND SAVE –

CHARLIE.	JAMIE.
Jesus!	God damn it I hate capitalism!

CHARLIE. Hold on I'm muting the ad! *(They do.)* Shit they've got the Verizon guy doing Sprint now? That's cold...

JAMIE. Is it almost –?

CHARLIE. Done.

> *(The soothing sound of a gentle rainstorm.*)*

JAMIE. ...Okay, not bad. Definitely more rain than jazz, but not bad.

> **(CHARLIE** *reaches for* **JAMIE***'s hand, gently reconnecting. They listen to the rain.)*

CHARLIE. Do you want to start the timer?

> **(JAMIE** *and* **CHARLIE** *begin touching. It starts soft and slow and tender, tracing each other's outlines with their fingertips as they cautiously rediscover each other.)*

How PG do we have to keep it again?

JAMIE. Just kissing and touching this week. Next week we can start rounding more of the bases.

CHARLIE. I haven't used baseball metaphors in a minute.

JAMIE. I know it's dumb –

CHARLIE. I like it. Gives us the chance to appreciate every step.

> *(They kiss.)*

(Flirty.) It might be kind of difficult to control myself though...

JAMIE. *(Tensing up.)* Um –

CHARLIE. Oh – I didn't mean it like –

---

*A license to produce *Slow Jam* does not include a performance license for any third-party or copyrighted recordings. Licensees should create their own.

JAMIE. No I know.

CHARLIE. I just meant –

JAMIE. It's fine.

CHARLIE. – That I miss this. I miss you.

JAMIE. I know and I feel really bad about that.

CHARLIE. Don't feel bad, I meant it as a good thing.

> (JAMIE*'s breath becomes shallow.*)

Like obviously feel what you feel, I'm not telling you how to feel I just – are you okay?

JAMIE. Yeah – yeah I'm fine.

> (JAMIE *takes a big sip of their drink.*)

CHARLIE. Hey, we really don't have to do this.

JAMIE. I'm fine, I promise.

CHARLIE. Are you sure?

JAMIE. FUCK – the timer's still going! Shit-shit-shit – how many seconds do you think that was?

CHARLIE. I think it's okay if it's not exactly –

JAMIE. The therapist said it has to be ten minutes, physical connection without sex for ten minutes.

CHARLIE. Why don't we take a break for a second?

JAMIE. No we're doing this. Let's just keep going.

> (JAMIE *resumes the timer and doubles down, determined. They kiss* CHARLIE *intensely – almost aggressively.* CHARLIE *pulls away.*)

CHARLIE. Hold on –

JAMIE. No I can do this, I promise.

(JAMIE kisses them again, harder.)

CHARLIE. Jamie, stop. Stop!

JAMIE. What?!

CHARLIE. What are you doing?

JAMIE. We said we would do this.

CHARLIE. Not if it's hurting you.

JAMIE. You're not the one who hurt me.

CHARLIE. But you're clearly not okay –

JAMIE. You don't get to decide if I'm okay.

CHARLIE. Okay then I don't want to do it!

JAMIE. Fine!

> *(CHARLIE stops the rain. JAMIE goes to the end of the bed, tucking their knees to their chest.)*
>
> *(The cats meow loudly outside the door.)*
>
> *(JAMIE takes a breath and comes back into their body.)*

CHARLIE. I'm sorry.

JAMIE. Me too.

CHARLIE. You don't have to apologize.

JAMIE. No, I do. PTSD doesn't mean you can be an asshole.

CHARLIE. Asshole might be a little intense.

JAMIE. *(An exhausted joke, an apology.)* Okay then I'm sorry you can't handle the intensity of my asshole.

CHARLIE. *(Accepting the apology.)* Stop flirting with me.

JAMIE. Literally never.

(The cats meow louder and scratch at the door.)

CHARLIE. We never should have registered them as emotional support animals, it went straight to their heads.

JAMIE. They just don't like when they can hear us but can't get to us.

CHARLIE. Tiny fuzzy little dictators.

JAMIE. You know the solution to this problem?

CHARLIE. Is it more Rain / and Jazz?

JAMIE. It's more Rain and Jazz.

> *(**JAMIE** presses play again. They listen together, but their bodies remain separate and guarded.)*

It's not fair that things that happened before we even met could still – I don't know. I get that "fair" isn't really part of it, I just – I don't want to have to go away to be close to you.

CHARLIE. We don't have to do anything. We can go for the "coffee shop or study session" Rain and Jazz experience.

JAMIE. But I miss you too.

CHARLIE. I mean...I'm not going anywhere.

> *(**CHARLIE** reaches out their hand, and **JAMIE** takes it. They stay like this for a moment.)*

CHARLIE. Did the therapist say we *had* to use a timer?

JAMIE. I think they technically just said it had to be ten minutes.

CHARLIE. What would you think about maybe just looking at the clock –

JAMIE. – Instead of a stopwatch counting down to the conclusion of our intimacy? Yeah no I get that.

(A cheesy saxophone solo abruptly blares over the rain. Think George Michael's "Careless Whisper."*)

CHARLIE. Who mixed this?!

JAMIE. Wow yeah that is entirely unforgivable.

(CHARLIE turns off the music.)

At least we tried.

CHARLIE. We did.

(They put their phones to the side and cuddle up, no longer trying to initiate anything, just simply being together.)

JAMIE. Maybe we could try a little less next time?

CHARLIE. I'll follow your lead.

(The cats scream and throw their bodies against the door.)

Should we let them in?

JAMIE. Not just yet.

(JAMIE blows out the candle and crawls back into bed.)

End of Play

---

*A license to produce *Slow Jam* does not include a performance license for any third-party or copyrighted music. Licensees should create an original composition or use music in the public domain. For further information, please see Music and Third-Party Materials Use Note on page iii.

The Falling Man

Gethsemane Herron

THE FALLING MAN premiered on February 20, 2017 at the Columbia School of the Arts MFA in Playwriting program, in the Schapiro Theater. The production was directed by Katherine Wilkinson and dramaturged by Blossom Johnson. The cast was as follows:

LEYLA...Manuela Sosa
CARRIE ....Candace Boahene
MAN / JOURNALIST ....Odera Adimorah

THE FALLING MAN was produced in the ninth annual The Fire This Time Festival. It premiered on January 15, 2018. The production was directed by Candis C. Jones. The cast was as follows:

LEYLA.......................................Ashley Marie Ortiz
CARRIE ....Lauren F. Walker
JOURNALIST ....Kevin Necciai
MAN...Kambi Gathesha

CHARACTERS

LEYLA – twenties, Latina, Pious and Confused

CARRIE – twenties, Black, Fierce and so very young

MAN / JOURNALIST – late thirties/early forties, Brave, Dark Brown Skin

SETTING

New York City

TIME

September 11, 2001

October 2001

To Eddie Herron, Sr.
Wherever you are, I hope you are free.

Scene One

(Nothing but black – overwhelming, smothering black. The air made dry by dust. It should billow, get under the nails. It should be impossible to shake off.)

(At Rise: A dim light emerges from upstage center. A building – a shortened skyscraper. On top of it, a **MAN** *in a white shirt stands. He falls forward. He tumbles. Until he hangs vertically by his ankles. A camera's flash. He is lowered to the ground. He leaves. His vertical image remains projected,* but his face – it's blurred by the glare.* **CARRIE** *and* **LEYLA** *enter. They do not look at the image. They do not look at each other.)*

CARRIE.	LEYLA.
I'm telling you right now.	I'm telling you right now.
That's not him.	That's not him.
That man is not my father.	That man is not my father.

(They leave. We are left with the man, his sole horizontal with the sky.)

---

*A license to produce *The Falling Man* does not include a license to publicly display any third-party or copyrighted images. Licensees must acquire rights for any copyrighted images or create their own.

Scene Two

(The **WOMEN** *walk past the image. It burns into the perpendicular of their eyes, but they walk past it briskly. They are never on the same side.)*

CARRIE. It couldn't possibly be him.

LEYLA. He never wore white.

CARRIE. He was never on time. For him to have been there when –

LEYLA. When –

CARRIE. The falling. He'd have to be on time.

LEYLA. If he could help it.

CARRIE. Of all the days to change –

LEYLA. It washed him out.

CARRIE. Why this day?

LEYLA. *(Muttering to herself.)* "Our."

CARRIE. Shoulda stayed his ass home!

LEYLA. "Father."

CARRIE. Why move? You didn't have to move.

LEYLA. It couldn't possibly be him.

CARRIE. When –

LEYLA. He was never –

CARRIE. He could help it. Our father who –

LEYLA. Shoulda stayed his ass at home.

CARRIE. Our father –

LEYLA. Who art in heaven...

(Pause.)

CARRIE. *"Your* father...he was in...he might not come home."

LEYLA. My father, who art in heaven...

If you *are* in heaven, please stay there.

CARRIE. But if not, return to me.

LEYLA. Do not leave again.

(The picture disappears.)

Scene Three

(The **MAN** *appears, dressed as a* **JOURNALIST.** *He stands between the two* **WOMEN,** *center stage. He raises a balled fist and knocks.)*

JOURNALIST. Excuse me, miss –?

LEYLA. Yes.

JOURNALIST. Hello, I'm with the –

CARRIE. I know who you're with.

JOURNALIST. Would you answer some questions?

CARRIE. About?

JOURNALIST. Have you seen this photo?

(The photograph of the falling man reappears.*)

*(***LEYLA*** and ***CARRIE*** are both silent. Boil.)*

Ma'am? Have you seen this man? Do you know this man?

CARRIE. I –

JOURNALIST. Can you identify this man?

LEYLA. No hablo ingles.

JOURNALIST. Miss, I know this must be difficult.

LEYLA. Yo no se.

JOURNALIST. Miss, I know you understand me –

(Whistle.)

LEYLA. *(With defiance.)* Yo no se.

---

*A license to produce *The Falling Man* does not include a license to publicly display any third-party or copyrighted images. Licensees must acquire rights for any copyrighted images or create their own.

CARRIE. Understand this, I don't know that man.

JOURNALIST. Miss, you've barely looked –

    (Overflow.)

CARRIE. He wouldn't die that way.

LEYLA. My father –

CARRIE. He wouldn't leap into death –

LEYLA. He'd –

CARRIE. Like a bitch coming back from war –

LEYLA. He'd trick death –

CARRIE. My daddy didn't do wars, okay –

LEYLA. Not the other way around.

CARRIE. *My daddy stayed his ass home.*

LEYLA. Death ain't gonna sneak up on him –

CARRIE. He stayed!

LEYLA. He'd charm death –

CARRIE. Wouldn't believe that shit, just eat it all the Fuck up –

LEYLA. Convince death that he wasn't no damn good –

CARRIE. Death would fall for him, not the other way around.

LEYLA. Death deserved better than him.

CARRIE. He wouldn't die like that, so you can gon' head and leave because –

LEYLA.	**CARRIE.**
I'm telling you right now. That's not him. That man is not my father.	I'm telling you right now. That's not him. That man is not my father.

JOURNALIST. *(Pressing on.)* Miss, it's October 12. Have you seen your father this last month?

LEYLA. My father would be where he always has been. Still. But not absent. Still. But not absent.

JOURNALIST. Miss, I can't understand you. I won't understand you. I can't. I don't understand your no.

LEYLA. It's not the death that matters, but how the dying's done.

JOURNALIST. Miss, I don't understand – there's not shame in jumping. They just needed to breathe. They aren't quitters because they needed to breathe.

LEYLA. They needed to fight. He needed to fight for me. How do you mourn a man who was only half there –

CARRIE. To begin with? But it was better than nothing.

LEYLA. It was better than this.

> *(Pause.)*

CARRIE. So, why should I talk to you, sir? Huh?

LEYLA. You gonna bring back the other half? Huh?

JOURNALIST. I'm a journalist.

> I don't run away.

> I keep looking.

> I run towards.

> It's what I do.

> I record so the people know.

LEYLA. People? I'm people? I get to be people now?

> You gon' bring back what was left?

CARRIE. You gon' bring back what was left?

LEYLA. If not...then I don't have much to say to you.

> *(The **JOURNALIST** exits.)*

> What language will you return in?

CARRIE. They are gonna find him.

LEYLA. How will I call you?

To whom do you answer to now?

CARRIE. I'm gonna get that half. I'm gonna get that half that's mine. I'ma get mine. I'ma get what's coming to me. What's coming back to me. I'm gonna –

LEYLA. What language am I supposed to mourn with?

Which language is the private home?

Which language is not my work clothes?

Can I sit on my bed in these outside clothes?

With this outsider's tongue?

Which language would he want me in?

(Pause.)

Would you sit with me? Would you sit with me? Would you sit with me? Will you tell me why you left my mother?

(She switches languages.)

Me dirás que hiciste con tu otra mitad?

Quien fue tu otra mitad?

A quien le diste tu otra mitad?

Que me dejaste?

Que compartimos?

Santa María, madre de dios

Madre de mi padre, mi abuela

Lo vas a castigar?

Will you tell me what you did with the other half?

Who was your other half?

Who did you give your other half to?

What did you leave me?

What did we share?

Hail Mary, mother of God,

Mother of my father, my grandmother,

Will you punish him...?

CARRIE. That's how it happened. He jumped. He flew. I'm sure the last ten seconds were glorious. I'm sure he thought about us. I'm sure the gold watch survived. God, if not the living man, not the half of a man, please let me have his watch. He really loved it.

>   (*Pause.*)

Oh, who am I kidding?

That watch is long gone.

>   (*Pause.*)

I wish he would have called.

At least.

LEYLA. For this one, great exit,

This one last sin?

He's gonna be okay, right?

You won't be too harsh?

You'll be merciful, right?

You'll be merciful...

CARRIE. I'd cherish a fingernail.

A toe, a toe, even.

>   (*The* JOURNALIST *re-enters at the site of the jumping. Ostensibly, he looks for clues. But as he comes back on to the shortened skyscraper:*)

LEYLA & CARRIE. So, what do I do?

> *(The* **MAN** *takes off the journalist gear.)*

> *(The* **MAN** *is just a man.)*

> *(The* **MAN** *looks down at the mourning* **WOMEN.***)*

MAN. Shit. SHIT. Man, I knew I should have stayed my ass home today.

"Don't call out," my wife says.

"I hate it there," I say. Said, I hate it, serving these folks.

"I don't want to die serving these folk," I said. But she said, "Go. Go. It's $13.24 per hour."

And I thought that my body was worth more than $13.24 per hour, but hell, what do I know?

What do I know what my body is worth?

> *(He pauses, his breathing labored.)*

> *(The air should smell dry again.)*

I'd rather jump than burn.

I'd rather die breathing.

Hell, I'd rather die in bed.

The robbery of it.

My body is a fucking miracle.

> *(Pause.)*

I want to own it.

I want to be a Black man that owns his own damn body.

I want to be a Black man that owns his own damn body.

I want to be a Black man that owns his own damn body!

I want to be a Black man that owns his own damn body!

His own damn body. If only for ten seconds.

>   *(He looks around him, as if to look at his*
>   *peers – his fellow jumpers.)*

Tell my daughter I'm sorry.

I was only half of what she needed.

I was only partially there.

>   *(Pause.)*

Tell my wife I know she loves as best she can.

So, this is how I die. Trapped in a burning building. A paper building.

I gotta fucking die with my co-workers.

Ain't that some shit.

>   *(He looks around at the chaos of the day.)*

I think we were wrong.

I don't think heaven is a utopia.

Heaven was my daughter's hand.

When I hold her, I hold my very pulse.

I hold my voice box.

I hold my own hands when I taught her to walk.

I hold the proof that I was here.

I was real.

>   *(He steels himself.)*

I think it's time to go now.

>   *(He approaches the edge: the limbo.)*

If hell is this burning building...

(Lights off.)

Heaven is clean air.

(Blackout.)

End of Play

Voir Dire

Carissa Atallah

VOIR DIRE was presented at the John F. Kennedy Center for the Performing Arts as part of the 50th Annual Kennedy Center American College Theater Festival on April 18, 2019. It was directed by Katie Ciszek. The cast was as follows:

WOMAN 1 .... Nancy Robinette
WOMAN 2 .... Alexandra Palting
WOMAN 3 .... Irene Hamilton
WOMAN 4 .... Guadalupe Campos
GOVERNMENT WORKER .... Eric Messner
MAN 1, 2, 3, 4 .... Tyler Liams
Dan Poppen
Carlos Saldaña
Matthew Alan Ward

CHARACTERS

WOMAN 1 – (any adult age, any race/ethnicity, female) a devout wife and mother

WOMAN 2 – (late teens/early twenties, any race/ethnicity, female) a university student

WOMAN 3 – (any adult age, any race/ethnicity, female) a confident New Yorker

WOMAN 4 – (a mature adult, Latinx/o/a or Hispanic, Spanish-speaker, female) a woman claiming her voice

GOVERNMENT WORKER – (any adult age, any race/ethnicity, any gender) a bored government worker

MEN 1, 2, 3, 4 – (any adult age, any race/ethnicity, male) four average Joes

SETTING

A utilitarian room. In the room, there are eight chairs.
Four in back, dimly lit. And four in front, in the light.

(At rise, four **WOMEN,** *diverse in age, ethnicity, and style, occupy the front row of chairs. Four* **MEN** *occupy the rest of the chairs. There is something similar about each* **MAN,** *though it is difficult to put a finger on what.)*

(The voice of a bored **GOVERNMENT WORKER** *echoes from the other side of the room, close but far away. The voice calls "Juror Number..." followed by four numbers said simultaneously.)*

(All **WOMEN** *stand up, speaking as if to the back of the room.)*

WOMEN 1, 2 & 3. *(Variations of.)* Yeah, that's me.

GOVERNMENT WORKER. *(Voice-over.)* Have you, or anyone close to you, been sexually assaulted in your lifetime?

WOMAN 1. I'm sorry?

WOMAN 2. Have I...

WOMAN 3. What.

WOMAN 4. ...

GOVERNMENT WORKER. *(Voice-over.)* The question is, have you, or anyone close to you, been sexually assaulted in your lifetime?

WOMAN 1. Sorry, I wasn't expecting –

WOMAN 2. Um –

WOMAN 3. Yeah I heard ya the first time.

WOMAN 4. ...

GOVERNMENT WORKER. *(Voice-over.)* You need to answer before we can move on.

WOMAN 1. Sorry, but is this…necessary?

GOVERNMENT WORKER. *(Voice-over.)* If it's on the paper, that means it's necessary.

WOMAN 1. May I ask why?

GOVERNMENT WORKER. *(Voice-over, sighing.)* Say this was a case about a used-car salesman and a police officer. We've got to know, are you a used-car salesman? Are you married to a police officer? In the US, any person on trial is entitled to a fair and impartial jury.

WOMAN 3. So it's a sexual assault case. I knew it. So many sick fucks in this city.

WOMAN 2. Um.

GOVERNMENT WORKER. *(Voice-over.)* Yes?

WOMAN 2. What do you mean by "sexual assault," exactly?

(The sound of papers rustling.)

GOVERNMENT WORKER. *(Voice-over, reading.)* Sexual assault is any type of sexual contact or behavior that occurs without the explicit consent of the recipient. Falling under the definition of sexual assault are sexual activities such as forced sexual intercourse, forcible sodomy, child molestation, incest, fondling, and attempted rape.

WOMAN 2. Contact or behavior? Can't that mean a lot of things?

WOMAN 3. Wait, you're telling me all incest is rape? I'm thinking, hear me out here, what if as adults I consensually blow my big brother? Like *Game of Thrones.* I mean, that's hypothetical, of course, I don't actually have a big brother. Always wanted one though. Not to blow. But to go camping and stuff.

GOVERNMENT WORKER. *(Voice-over.)* Look, I don't write the definitions. I just need you to answer the question to the best of your ability.

WOMAN 1. Okay.

WOMAN 2. Okay.

WOMAN 3. But it's a stupid fucking question. I'm a woman. This is New York. A better question would be – who do I know that hasn't been assaulted?

WOMAN 1. Excuse me, sorry, but this is all confidential, right?

GOVERNMENT WORKER. *(Voice-over.)* Of course.

WOMAN 2. I don't wanna be throwing words like "sexual assault" around when I'm not exactly sure. I wanna say...maybe, no. Or...

GOVERNMENT WORKER. *(Voice-over.)* I can't do much with "maybe."

WOMAN 2. Sorry it's just...I'm still a little fuzzy on the details.

WOMAN 1. And it was a LONG time ago.

WOMAN 3. Just last week.

WOMAN 2. Maybe I could just...explain? And then you can decide for yourself.

GOVERNMENT WORKER. *(Voice-over.)* Go on.

WOMAN 2. I knew he had...um, non-friend kinda feelings for me. I'm good at picking up on those things. Sometimes you just have to pretend like you don't notice and hope it'll go away eventually. I lived in the dorms, but he lived in this house...with his older cousin and, at the end of the semester, they threw a kickback. Maybe not a kickback, maybe more like a party, and I've drank before but never that much and that's when, um, that's when I get not-so-sure.

GOVERNMENT WORKER. *(Voice-over.)* Ma'am? Ma'am, do you understand the question?

WOMAN 4. Yes.

GOVERNMENT WORKER. *(Voice-over.)* Yes you've been sexually assaulted, or yes you understand the question?

WOMAN 4. ...

WOMAN 1. My husband asked if I'd like to go steady with him the day I turned eighteen. I remember, gosh, was I relieved. I always thought, always feared, he might ask my sister first. Lidia was two years older than me. Twenty at the time. Closer to his age and what have you. But he always tells me, he says, "I would have waited as long as it took for you." I mention this because, I just want you to know, he isn't a bad guy. He's a real good man, a godly man.

GOVERNMENT WORKER. *(Voice-over.)* Okay –

WOMAN 3. So I'm jogging down to the Starbucks on the corner. Normally I don't bother with those chains, ya know? Heartless corporations, et cetera et cetera, but I'm in a rush. So I'm in line, right? And the barista calls "grande mocha frap no whip" and this dude, this grande-mocha-frap-no-whip-mother-fucker grabs MY ass on his way to the counter. And before I get a chance to say a thing, he's out the door.

WOMAN 2. I don't remember everything. But I remember moving from room to room to avoid him. And I remember crying, at some point. A lot. God, I'm so embarrassing. Being that girl at the party. But yeah, crying and repeating..."I can't breath. I can't breath." I had anxiety. Well, have...anxiety.

WOMAN 3. And I get it, my ass looks pretty damn grabbable in spandex. So I'm not even that shy about people touching it. What's mine is yours, ya know? But have the decency to ask first. Fuck. The whole thing basically ruined my morning. I mean, he – he –

WOMAN 1. – He was the youth group leader of the teen ministry. Twenty-five when I was seventeen. Which is completely arbitrary, isn't it? My mom was fourteen when she met my father, and they've been together thirty years in counting. But I guess that's the difference, isn't it?

Between New York and Alabama.

WOMAN 3. You know what? I bet he's some pretentious jerk who thinks he's cutting calories by not adding whip, as if the Frappuccino alone isn't a week's worth of sugar. As if the whip cream ain't the best fucking part. Hey – are you even listening?

(*Beat.*)

GOVERNMENT WORKER. (*Voice-over.*) Well, are you? Are you even listening?

WOMAN 4. Yes, I am a-listening.

GOVERNMENT WORKER. (*Voice-over.*) And you understand?

WOMAN 2. I can't say that I understand entirely. Because he did the right thing, all right? He asked, at some point, anyway, if this was okay. But it still doesn't feel okay. I –

WOMAN 1. – I asked him to give me a ride home one day after group. He said yes, but instead he drove me out to the fields where they do the pumpkin patch for the harvest festival.

WOMAN 2. That I remember. His breath on my face. Smelling like vodka and Red Bull. His hands already on my waste, frustrated that the jeans I was wearing that night had buttons instead of a zip.

WOMAN 1. He pulled off to the side of the road and asked me if I'd ever seen a man below-the-waist before. I thought, maybe this was some sort of confession, so I said yes, we all had, in the videos on Marcy's older brother's laptop. And he said, "How about in person?" and I shook my head. And he said, "Would you like to see mine?" Now, let's make one thing clear –

WOMEN 1 & 2. I never said no.

WOMAN 3. I said no way am I letting that guy get away with this crap any longer. So I started going to that same Starbucks, real regular. And let me tell you, I am quite the vigilante because I musta gained ten pounds that month on pound cake alone.

WOMAN 1. Alone, I don't think that I touched him for more than two seconds before he jumped out of the car. He knelt down right on the side of the road. Do you know what he was doing?

GOVERNMENT WORKER. *(Voice-over.)* I can only imagine.

WOMAN 1. Why he was praying, repenting. Asking the good Lord to forgive him for giving in to my temptation. And now I know, I know technically what he did –

WOMAN 2. – Technically what I did was consensual. It just didn't feel that way, you know? Didn't feel like I had much of a choice at all. And he knew I had a hard time, with the anxiety, with the saying "no" part, and yeah he was drunk. That's his great excuse. But I was way drunker.

WOMEN 1, 2 & 3. And you wanna know what?

GOVERNMENT WORKER. *(Voice-over.)* What?

WOMAN 1. If I were a year or two older, it wouldn't make a lick of difference. Well, age isn't everything, and I may be a woman, but I don't like to play myself the victim 'til the cows come home. Besides, I didn't see him for a long time after that. He was off doing mission work, in Ghana, and when he got back, I was eighteen, and he told me he was in love with me all along. And now, now I have a good Christian husband who'd do anything,

anything at all for our two girls, and he loves them with all his heart so really, really I don't think I was ever assaulted, and I hate feminists for always trying to convince me different.

WOMAN 2. So whatever, okay, I wake up still drunk the next morning. I'm on this couch, the same couch where it happened, and my roommate is shaking me saying, "It's time to get up. Are you crying? What's wrong?" And I feel my face, and I am crying, and I don't know what to say 'cept, "I let people do things to me that I don't want to do." And that's it. I say that again and again, and you know what? To this day, he doesn't think he did anything wrong. Girls just don't date nice guys. He was friend-zoned, or whatever. And I haven't – with anyone – since. And sometimes I just wish that I had been unconscious. Then, at least, I wouldn't remember. Then, at least I'd know for sure that it wasn't my fault. That there was nothing I could do – that it really was – really was –

WOMAN 3. I'm a freelance digital consultant, so I'm real work-on-the-go. Who needs an office, ya know? So I'm sitting there with my cold brew, same time'a day like three times a week, and eventually I see the mother-fucker in action! Reaches right up the skirt of some toddler. Okay, maybe I shouldn't say toddler, cuz that woulda been, Christ, something else, but let's just say there's no way this girl was old enough to have voted the first black president into office. Not even second-term. And the poor thing, she didn't know what to do. But you bet your ass I did! I dumped my drink over his head! I'm thinking, that will show him! But here's the thing, turns out...he owns the entire block. And now would ya believe it, I'm not allowed at the Starbucks off Lincoln anymore. Whatever. This is New York. Not like I'm short of coffee shop options, am I right? Gotta say though, I'll miss their lemon sugar pound cake. That's for damn sure.

WOMAN 4. Cuando éramos jóvenes, mi hermana era la chica más hermosa del pueblo. Quizás el mundo. Ella significaba todo para mí. Ella tenía varios pretendientes, pero decidió esperar hasta que me casara primero. Porque yo era la mayor. Ella siempre fue muy considerada. Entonces, un día, algunos soldados llegaron al pueblo. Y las cosas que le hicieron a ella. Las cosas que los vi hacer. Pude haberles arrancado el escroto y dárselos de comer como sopa de albóndigas. Ojalá y lo tuviera hecho. Ningún hombre la volviera a tocar después de eso. Ella murió después de eso.

GOVERNMENT WORKER. *(Voice-over.)* Lady, lady –

> *(Beat.)*

Thank you for your time. But you've been considered unfit for these proceedings. You may go.

> *(The **WOMEN** shrug or pick up their purses or straighten their skirts and go.)*

> *(The voice of the bored **GOVERNMENT WORKER** echoes from the other side of the room, close but far away. It calls "Juror Number..." then four numbers at once. Together, they are nearly indecipherable.)*

> *(All four **MEN** stand up and replace the women where they stood.)*

Have you, or anyone close to you, been sexually assaulted in your lifetime?

ALL MEN. *(Variations of.)* Not that I know of / no.

> *(Curtain.)*

End of Play

I Didn't Think You'd Be So Unhappy

Shara Feit

I DIDN'T THINK YOU'D BE SO UNHAPPY was originally developed in The Lark's 2018-2019 Staff/Apprentice Writers' group and subsequently developed in The Frauds, an interdisciplinary writers' group.

I DIDN'T THINK YOU'D BE SO UNHAPPY was workshop-produced in Williamstown Theatre Festival's 5x10 Series on June 26, 2019. The production was directed by Michael Herwitz, with costume design by Maddie Kevelson, lighting design by Maggie Ste. Marie, sound design by Jessica Sell, and prop design by Laura Chandler Robinson. The cast was as follows:

JULES . . . . Olivia Atwood

REBECCA . . . . Lilla Brody

THE BAT MITZVAH GIRL . . . . Kaitlyn Gonzalez

CHARACTERS

JULES – mid-to-late twenties, woman
REBECCA – mid-to-late twenties, woman
THE BAT MITZVAH GIRL – 12, young woman

SETTING

The back alley of a synagogue, probably reform or conservative,
likely not orthodox. The bat mitzvah inside is modern orthodox or
conservative.

TIME

Now-ish or the kind of now-ish that is a lot like 2007 because really,
haven't bat mitzvahs basically been the same since the '90s?

AUTHOR'S NOTES

On Formatting

A dash "-" indicates a cutoff.

[Square brackets] are thoughts and intentions communicated using
sounds that are not words.

Within dialogue, *italicized* text is emphatic, and text in ALL CAPS is
explosive. Emphasized and explosive things are not always louder,
though they sometimes are.

Line breaks are there to help navigate breaks in thought. Sometimes
those breaks are miniscule, though, so don't let them slow you down
unless you've reached a moment of breath in the play. Same goes for
pauses. And on that note...

On Pace

This play moves fast. Things are funny until they aren't, and maybe even
then they are still kinda funny.

On Casting

No version of this play exists with an all-white cast. Lots of party
motivators and bat mitzvah girls are women of color.

Cast color consciously. Also, the bat mitzvah girl doesn't have to be
played by an actual twelve-year-old.

"Sixth-grade boys are the stupidest people in the world. But sixth-grade girls are the meanest." – My Dad

(The back alley of a synagogue. By some huge garbage bins. Maybe it smells like yesterday's herring and leftovers and car exhaust.)

(Inside, the music is bumping, the chocolate fountain is flowing, the kiddies are chugging Shirley Temples, the teens are pretending to be twenty-one and too cool for this shit, the adults are drinking [inappropriately] heavily, the divorced relatives are either whisper-yelling or glaring at each other from across the room, and the middle school girls are waging emotional warfare and popping pimples and squeezing two thousand gallons of gloss onto their lips.)*

(Close to one hundred pre-teenagers are dancing, shuffling with their hands in their pockets, and generally destroying their immediate surroundings.)

(You know what it is, kids.)

(It's a

GOSH

DARN

BAT FRIGGIN' MITZVAH.)

---

*A license to produce *I Didn't Think You'd Be So Unhappy* does not include a performance license for any third-party or copyrighted music. Licensees should create an original composition or use music in the public domain. For further information, please see Music and Third-Party Materials Use Note on page iii.

(But we're not inside, honey. We're not so lucky, or cursed, depending on your understanding of the sitch. But we do hear it – the murmurs, the energy, the dreams and the worst nightmares, the pulsing combination of top-forty pop, circle dances, and bat mitzvah classics.*)

*(**JULES** and **REBECCA**, two party motivators wearing super-high heels and tight black clothes that also somehow conform to Jewish modesty standards, stand in the alley, eating, on a five.)*

JULES. *(While shoving food into her mouth.)* and i was like, "mark, no, we are absolutely not fucking in the boiler room of this synagogue that is an egregious idea."

REBECCA. yeah, duh.

JULES. clearly *not duh* because he was all "what does egregious mean?"

REBECCA. oh, mark.

JULES. so i was all: mark, your limited vocabulary aside, i'm going to remind you this is a Synagogue. it is not Just Another Place For You To Wave Around Your Penis. there are TORAHS here.

Do you even know what the torah is, mark? it is a very holy book for the jewish people. the torah is the reason we have jobs. so Respect The Fucking Torah.

also, we have to distribute glow sticks *right now* or timmy's gonna freak and we're both going to be fired.

also, i'm gay.

---

*A license to produce *I Didn't Think You'd Be So Unhappy* does not include a performance license for any third-party or copyrighted music. Licensees should create an original composition or use music in the public domain. For further information, please see Music and Third-Party Materials Use Note on page iii.

REBECCA. you are truly this poor man's worst nightmare.

JULES. HONESTLY i sleep with a man ONE TIME –

REBECCA. ha.

JULES. and the universe is so clearly like NOPE.

REBECCA. yeah 'cause like it's *you*, jules.

JULES. the point: do not sleep with your colleagues, even after a bar mitzvah headlined by nicki minaj.

REBECCA. noted.

JULES. ugggghhhh i ate too fast ughhhh i always do that. feels disgusting. but take it from me, when you stop to breathe, when you take one fucking second, that's exactly when someone yells at you about dance socks.

REBECCA. dance socks?

JULES. socks with little beads on them. so you don't slip. while dancing.

REBECCA. people get mad about stuff like that?

JULES. it's an important day.

every part of it matters.

REBECCA. wow okay.

JULES. believe me, soon you'll know exactly what it takes to throw a perfect bat mitzvah.

you'll feel really fucking overeducated a lot of the time but you'll get used to it.

REBECCA. *(Flat.)* you make rent doing this?

JULES. in a weekend. easy.

REBECCA. *(Probably still flat or small.)* i don't really care about feeling overeducated if i'm making rent in a weekend.

i don't really care about feeling anything.

(Pause.)

REBECCA. thank you for getting me this job.

JULES. for you, anything. you feel good about the dances?

REBECCA. yeah, i think so.

JULES. you looked great. you have a beautiful quality to your movement.

REBECCA. ten years of ballet finally put to good use, i guess.

JULES. and you're hydrating?

REBECCA. yup.

JULES. just know you can ask me anything at any time.

REBECCA. great.

JULES. also, i know it's been a little while

since we've like

confided

but if you need to like talk or cry, or something

that's chill with me. more than chill. *welcome.*

REBECCA. thanks for the offer but i don't think i need to do that right now.

JULES. cool.

(Pause.)

REBECCA. is this a good one?

JULES. what?

REBECCA. a good bar mitzvah?

JULES. it's a bat.

REBECCA. sorry?

JULES. BAT mitzvah.

BAT. for a girl. who is becoming a woman.

bar is for a boy. who is becoming a man.

REBECCA. oh. got it.

JULES. this one's okay. six out of ten?

REBECCA. what's a ten?

JULES. well... obvi subjective but my all-time favorite was this musical theater bat mitzvah?

there were huge playbill posters everywhere with the bat mitzvah girl's face on them,

and she entered in this lavender tea-length dress to a remix of "seasons of love"

and tiff and i danced with her, just like grapevining, but this girl could not dance *at all*, like she couldn't. even.grapevine. she could *barely* do the cha-cha slide! and we all know mr. c gives very comprehensive instructions!!!

but then, after coke and pepsi and the montage and the bat mitzvah girl's cringy eight-minute performance of a broadway medley, all of her friends stood up, presented her with a super sparkly memory bottle and sang to her...

"because we knew you, stephanie, we have been changed for good."

REBECCA. that's so cute.

JULES. and it scanned so poorly!!! but I was like, crying? all of a sudden?

and it was just like,

girl, you are completely weird-looking

and perhaps you will never truly grow into your body

and being an actor is unforgiving as fuck

so i sincerely hope you find something else you care about

(Truly moved by the memory.) but you are so clearly loved

and that is a *beautiful* thing

i mean, if i had been loved like that, en masse, and so genuinely, maybe i would be a different person. a better person.

sorry, fuck, i'm so selfish, going on about all of my bullshit that doesn't even matter when you have real problems.

REBECCA. you have real problems.

i care about your problems.

> *(Pause.)*

JULES. *(Genuine, loving.)* i know this obviously isn't what you planned or what you wanted.

it's not that for me either.

but i'm really glad you're here.

i really missed you.

> *(**REBECCA** kisses **JULES**.)*
>
> *(It's impulsive and weird and sort of stunning for them both.)*
>
> *(They break apart.)*
>
> *(Silence.)*
>
> *(Then **REBECCA** laughs.)*

REBECCA. sorry

it's just

you taste like the chocolate fountain.

JULES. why did you do that?

REBECCA. um

i wanted to?

JULES. i feel sick.

(**JULES** *vomits.*)

(**REBECCA** *instinctively holds her hair back.*)

REBECCA. whoa. um. okay. you're okay.

(**JULES** *stops vomiting, wipes her mouth.*)

i haven't held your hair back since high school. have you been sneaking themed cocktails without telling me?

JULES. i'm a Professional, i don't drink at work.

REBECCA. *(A joke.)* maybe you're pregnant, haha.

(Mini-pause.)

JULES. *(Realizing.)* oh my god.

REBECCA. *(Realizing, too.)* oh

shit.

(**JULES** *promptly begins to panic.*)

(*Enter* **THE BAT MITZVAH GIRL,** *the door slamming loudly behind her.*)

(**THE BAT MITZVAH GIRL** *is a waking nightmare in a blue gown and matching blue eyeshadow. Her mascara is running. She has clearly been crying.*)

THE BAT MITZVAH GIRL. what the fuck are you looking at.

REBECCA. um.

THE BAT MITZVAH GIRL. shouldn't you be, like, inside?

JULES. oh my god.

REBECCA. shouldn't you? it's your bat mitzvah.

JULES. ONE TIME!!!! AGHHHHHHHHH!!!

THE BAT MITZVAH GIRL. is she having a nervous breakdown?

REBECCA. likely.

THE BAT MITZVAH GIRL. whatever. my parents aren't paying for your quarter-life crises. they're paying for me to have the best night of my life because i am a Woman in the Eyes of God.

JULES. WHAT AM I GOING TO DO?

REBECCA. we're taking a five-minute break, we'll be back in soon.

THE BAT MITZVAH GIRL. is that vomit?

REBECCA. yes.

THE BAT MITZVAH GIRL. is that *her* vomit?

REBECCA. yes.

THE BAT MITZVAH GIRL. gross. she's gross.

REBECCA. vomiting is a natural, physiological thing –

THE BAT MITZVAH GIRL. she's vile. vomiting in an alley.

(*Repulsed beyond repulsed.*) she's trash. *disgusting*.

(*Pause.*)

REBECCA. you know what, judgy bat mitzvah girl?!

JULES. rebecca.

THE BAT MITZVAH GIRL. what?

REBECCA. I'LL TELL YOU.

JULES. please don't.

REBECCA. i'll have you know, being a woman is fucking disgusting sometimes!!!

THE BAT MITZVAH GIRL. i know about periods. i already got my period. at eleven.

REBECCA. i'm not talking about periods YOU NEOPHYTE –

THE BAT MITZVAH GIRL. what are you –

REBECCA. I'M TALKING ABOUT ALL OF WOMANHOOD.

JULES. *(Panicking.)* bec, you're freaking her out i really need this job –

REBECCA. there's blood, yes, but also guts and sweat and *vomit* and terrible choices and wasted time and sinking feelings in your stomach and heartbreak and so much pain and that's just it. it's messy and it hurts.

welcome.

but maybe, if you're lucky, you'll have a friend like her.

and that makes it easier.

(Silence.)

THE BAT MITZVAH GIRL. my best friend is kissing the guy i like.

right now.

his name is jake. he smells like axe body spray.

he uses too much axe body spray. but i like it.

he plays the french horn. badly. but i like that, too.

he's really smart. he draws doodles of birds and clouds and sometimes i look over his shoulder in class and imagine that we're flying somewhere warm together on the back of a huge, multicolored egret. he seems to have a very rich inner life for a thirteen-year-old boy?

i straightened my hair for him. i practiced walking in heels.

i thought i'd walk into the room and he would see me. *really* see me.

and he would melt. and i would melt. and we would both be nothing but liquid and glitter and sweat on the floor of my synagogue social hall, swirling into each other, making colors and patterns that no one had ever seen before.

and it wouldn't matter that i messed up my haftorah and my parents totally are getting a divorce, they're trying to hide it but i *know* it's happening, and that i have a pimple growing right now, i can feel it under my skin, and that sometimes all i want to do is scream and scream and scream and rip all of my skin off and scream some more but with all of my internal organs and blood and lymph hanging out!!!!

but instead of *seeing* me, he kissed my best friend.

at *my* bat mitzvah.

and, i'm like, a woman now, in the eyes of My Tradition.

(Desperate.) what do you think it all means?

> *(Pause.)*

REBECCA. oh honey.

we can't tell you anything about anything.

JULES. you should write poetry.

THE BAT MITZVAH GIRL. poetry is for losers, i want to write eviscerating intersectional feminist cultural criticism.

JULES. are your parents like professors?

THE BAT MITZVAH GIRL. no, why?

JULES. just wondering.

THE BAT MITZVAH GIRL. are you happy?

REBECCA.	JULES.
no.	today, not so much.

THE BAT MITZVAH GIRL. you're both so pretty.

> *(A big fucking discovery.)* i didn't think you'd be so unhappy.

> *(Pause.)*

REBECCA. it's not, like, *forever*

> the way you feel

> the way we feel

> it's just right now

> i hope you know that.

THE BAT MITZVAH GIRL. i should go back in.

> my parents are very anxious people.

JULES. wait.

> *(**JULES** takes some makeup wipes out of her purse.)*

> let's get that mascara off your cheeks, ya freaky smart cultural criticism girl.

THE BAT MITZVAH GIRL. Woman.

JULES. Woman.

> that's right.

> *(**JULES** wipes the mascara off **THE BAT MITZVAH GIRL**'s cheeks.)*

> good as new.

THE BAT MITZVAH GIRL. sorry for calling you disgusting.

JULES. you're forgiven, Mazel Tov.

THE BAT MITZVAH GIRL. there's mouthwash in the hospitality baskets in the bathroom

for like the vomit.

JULES. that's very considerate, go redeem your party!

THE BAT MITZVAH GIRL. *(Resolute.)* i'm going to pour a shirley temple down my ex-best friend's dress.

WITH the maraschino cherries!!

REBECCA. maybe don't punish another woman –

THE BAT MITZVAH GIRL. it's my party i can do what i want!!!!

>   *(And* **THE BAT MITZVAH GIRL** *is gone.)*
>
>   *(Silence.)*

JULES. do you think we should um

stop her?

REBECCA. no

let her live.

she'll learn.

JULES. you know you're like an actual maniac.

"blood and GUTS and PUKE. WOMANHOOD." that was crazy!!!!

REBECCA. you're my best friend.

i'd scream at a twelve-year-old in a gown for you any day.

>   *(Pause.)*

JULES. sorry i vomited after [you kissed me].

REBECCA. i must be a really terrible kisser.

JULES. *(All love.)* fuck you.

>   *(Pause.)*

sorry but i really don't want to date though, like i love you but –

REBECCA. girl, don't worry about it

it wasn't like that.

JULES. so why did you...

(Pause.)

REBECCA. i dunno

i guess i didn't have words for how it feels to be loved by someone, the way *you* –

and i've been thinking a lot about like what love is

love before it gets all twisted up and like ugly and hurts you and takes all your time

and i feel stupid for not being full-body *grateful* all the time

for not *telling* you how grateful –

so i felt like reminded and chastised

and like my whole body was made of gratitude and like love molecules, or something?

i didn't have words for it

or to thank you

still don't, really

clearly

still feel stupid

so yeah i just

[kissed you]

yeah.

(Silence.)

JULES. *(The real shit.)* i'm sorry i didn't *do anything*

 i'm sorry i didn't attack your stupid fucking ex

 i should have *done* something

 punched him in his dumb face

 something

 i failed you

 and i am so, so sorry.

REBECCA. it wasn't your job to – no one was gonna get me out until i was ready to get myself out

 and like

 i'm okay. you know? i'm gonna pay my rent and get, like, houseplants...

 i'm alive.

 i'm gonna be okay.

  (Pause.)

 (An offering, gentle.) you want me to come with you?

JULES. um where?

REBECCA. the drugstore, the doctor...wherever.

JULES. oh.

 yeah.

 i'd like that.

  (From inside, music plays.)*

 mr. c calls.

---

*A license to produce *I Didn't Think You'd Be So Unhappy* does not include a performance license for any third-party or copyrighted music. Licensees should create an original composition or use music in the public domain. For further information, please see Music and Third-Party Materials Use Note on page iii.

REBECCA. at least he gives comprehensive instructions.

JULES. good thing someone does.

(*Pause.*)

did you believe what you said? that it's not, like, forever?

REBECCA. i dunno

i hope so.

JULES. yeah

i hope so too.

(*The music gets louder.*)

let's dance?

REBECCA. let's dance.

End of Play

Masking Our
Blackness

Vincent Terrell Durham

MASKING OUR BLACKNESS premiered at Highways Performance Space on July 27, 2018, presented by McCormick/Durham and Highways Performance Space (Leo Garcia, Executive Director & Patrick Kennelly, Artistic Director). The production was directed by Rondrell McCormick, with set design by Rondrell McCormick, costumes by Wendell C. Carmichael, and lighting design by Kenneth Cosby. The stage manager was Jacob St. Aubin. The cast was as follows:

DARRYL. . . . . Nic Few

SIMON. . . . . .Jon Joseph Gentry

CARA . . . . .Angela K. Thomas

RICHARD . . . . Gerard W.A. Joseph II

SAMARIA. . . . . Rachael Ferrera

CHARACTERS

DARRYL – Black-American, male, 24 to 35

SIMON – Black-American, male, 24 to 35

CARA – Black-American, female, 24 to 35

RICHARD – Black-American, male, 24 to 35

SAMARIA – Black-American, female, 24 to 35

SETTING

The home of Darryl and Samaria in Anywhere, USA

TIME

It's New Year's Eve of the year before the play is being performed.

(At Rise: The couple, **DARRYL** *and* **SAMARIA,** *and their friends* **RICHARD, SIMON,** *and* **CARA** *gather around to welcome in the New Year.)*

DARRYL. Ten seconds to midnight everybody!

SIMON. Let's do this.

ALL. Ten-nine-eight-seven-six-five-four-three-two-one HAPPY NEW YEAR!

> *(***DARRYL** *and* **SAMARIA** *kiss, and both start singing "Aud Lang Syne."* **SIMON** *and* **RICHARD** *exchange high-fives.* **CARA** *celebrates.)*

CARA. We made it! We made it everybody! Happy New Year! Happy 2020!

DARRYL. Happy New Year!

RICHARD. Happy New Year, Brotha.

SAMARIA. Resolutions! Resolutions, everyone! We are just a few seconds into a brand-new year and that means brand-new hopes and brand-new dreams for everybody. Who wants to go first?

CARA. I resolve to lose my last ten pounds of post-baby weight.

> *(Everyone cheers their support.)*

SAMARIA. Hold up. You ain't never had a baby.

SIMON. She meant post-eating weight.

RICHARD. She also meant twenty-five pounds.

CARA. Damn. I thought I was with friends, but y'all ain't stealing my joy. I'll be attending Zumba classes on

Mondays and Fridays. Taking Hip-Hop Ab classes every Tuesday, Wednesday and Thursday, with that fine-ass instructor Malik –

DARRYL. *(Dismissing **CARA**'s resolution.)* Good luck. NEXT!

SIMON. I resolve to –

CARA. Can a Sistah finish?

SIMON. My bad. What else you got?

CARA. Not to get shot and killed by the police.

RICHARD. Are you serious?

SIMON. She can't be serious.

SAMARIA. Girl, I was with you right up to Hip-Hop Ab classes. Seeing Malik's fine ass three times a week is a resolution any woman can keep.

DARRYL. *(Warning **SAMARIA**.)* Careful, Baby. Careful.

SIMON. None of us should be trying to make that resolution.

RICHARD. I give you until February.

CARA. To drop ten pounds?

RICHARD. No, until you get shot and killed by the police. My boy Tyrone made that same resolution last year. Six hours into the new year he was shot twenty-two times by one cop. Who has a real resolution? One they can actually keep.

SIMON. I resolve to no longer purchase articles of clothing that make me appear suspicious or threatening. I also resolve to cross the street whenever a white woman is approaching me.

DARRYL. So she won't think you're going to try and steal her pocketbook.

SIMON. You feel my pain, Brotha?

(**SIMON** *and* **DARRYL** *exchange high-fives.*)

RICHARD. Every Black man has felt that pain.

SAMARIA. I don't see you giving up your Timberlands.

CARA. And saggin'. Your pants haven't been around your waist since the third grade. You've been considered suspicious and threatening ever since you turned eight.

SAMARIA. That's that school to prison pipeline.

SIMON. Wearing black or grey hoodies can get your ass shot. I'm saying goodbye to all that. I was recently approved for a Brooks Brothers' credit card.

ALL OTHERS. Brooks Brothers?

SIMON. It came in the mail three days ago. I got a seventy-five dollar limit.

SAMARIA. If you got a Brooks Brothers credit card in your pocket, why are you still dressed like a member of the Wu-Tang Clan rather than Ben Carson?

SIMON. Well, you see. What had happen was –

DARRYL. What had happen was – You walked your Wu-Tang Clan-looking ass up into Brooks Brothers and they thought you were there to rob the place.

SIMON. Not at all. Four people rushed to assist me as soon as I walked through the door.

RICHARD. Since when do security guards measure your inseam? That was stop and frisk, Man.

CARA. So why are you still dressed like what Fox and Friends would call a drug-dealing thug?

SIMON. There was a slight issue with the credit card.

ALL OTHERS. They didn't believe it was yours.

SIMON. Identity theft is a big problem these days.

SAMARIA. Why not pull out your driver's license and prove it was you?

SIMON. Hell no. With four security guards surrounding me? Remember the video of the brother pulling out his driver's license during a traffic stop? The cop shot his ass twenty-two times.

RICHARD. That was my boy Tyrone. His dash-cam video went viral! Two million views.

DARRYL. Y'all need to do better with these resolutions.

SIMON. We haven't heard from Richard.

(Everybody looks at **RICHARD.***)*

RICHARD. I stopped making resolutions three years ago.

SAMARIA. I remember that resolution.

CARA. That was the year you was trying to bring sexy back.

RICHARD. I was trying to train for the New York City Marathon.

CARA. All I know was by April a brotha had it going on.

SAMARIA. You were looking Michael B. Jordan kind of sexy.

CARA. Chadwick Boseman kind of sexy.

> (**CARA** *and* **SAMARIA** *exchange Black Panther salutes with each other and fall out in laughter.)*

CARA.	SAMARIA.
Wakanda forever!	Wakanda forever!

DARRYL. *(Warning* **SAMARIA.***)* Careful, Baby. Careful.

SIMON. Why did you stop training for that marathon?

RICHARD. White women.

DARRYL. Permit Patty?

SIMON. Central Park Karen?

DARRYL. Barbecue Becky?

RICHARD. All of the above. They kept calling 911 and reporting a Black man running through the neighborhood. It was my neighborhood before they moved in with their yoga mats. I'm done with resolutions. You can keep all that hope for a safer tomorrow.

SAMARIA. Don't bring us down, Richard. I think Darryl has a way for all of us to get through the new year without being shot and killed by the police. Honey, tell everyone what your New Year's resolutions are.

> (**DARRYL** *opens a large wooden box that sits on top of a table.*)

DARRYL. I resolve not to get stopped and frisked every time I walk down the street. I resolve not to get pulled over for a broken taillight on my brand-new car. I resolve not to get tased while shopping for toiletries at Walmart.

> (**DARRYL** *leans into the wooden box and places a white mask over his face. He returns to an upright position and has been transformed into a Caucasian man.*)

SIMON. Who invited the white dude?

CARA. I think it's Darryl.

SAMARIA. No, it's white Darryl. Doesn't he look wonderful?

> (**SAMARIA** *reaches into the wooden box and places a white mask over her own face and is transformed into a Caucasian woman.*)

SIMON. *(Shocked at **SAMARIA**'s transformation.)* What the fuck?

SAMARIA. We can drive through Texas without getting pulled over.

CARA. What about swimming pools? Can you go to a pool party without being thrown down to the ground?

SAMARIA. You can go to any swimming pool that you want to. You can even put your head underneath the water.

CARA. Give me one of those.

RICHARD. I want one too.

> (**RICHARD** *and* **CARA** *rush to the wooden box and pull out two white masks and place them over their faces. They are both transformed into Caucasians.* **SIMON** *stares at the unfolding scene.*)

I have a sudden desire to watch *Seinfeld*.

CARA. Something is telling me to put peas in my macaroni salad, and to leave my chicken unseasoned.

> (**SAMARIA** *pulls out two hand mirrors from the wooden box and hands one to* **CARA**. *They both admire their new reflections.*)

SAMARIA. Look at us. Have you ever felt prettier?

CARA. Never. We have good hair.

RICHARD. What's this feeling I'm having?

DARRYL. White male privilege, Bro. Demanding proof that someone lives in your apartment building. Arguing with a cop and still making it home alive.

RICHARD. I think I could get used to this.

SAMARIA. Darryl and I have been wearing our masks outside for a week. No labels. No judgments.

DARRYL. Not considered suspicious. Not considered a thug. We got the bathroom code from Starbucks without buying coffee. We actually brought in our own coffee.

SAMARIA. 94483 is the override code to every bathroom inside a Starbucks. It spells out W H I T E on the bathroom keypad. Only we get to use it.

(**DARRYL** *and* **SAMARIA** *exchange a low-five in celebration.*)

DARRYL. Down low!

(*All four begin relishing the experience and fully slip into their new whiteness.*)

CARA. It's beautiful being white.

RICHARD. Totally beautiful.

ALL BUT SIMON. Totally!

(**SIMON** *goes to the wooden box and searches for his mask.*)

SIMON. There's not one in here for me, Darryl. Samaria is there another mask?

DARRYL. Who is that?

SAMARIA. There's a colored man in our house.

CARA. Somebody call 911.

RICHARD. We'll be dead by the time 911 arrives. Let's give him some money or whatever he's looking for.

(*To* **SIMON.**) Do you need money for drugs?

SIMON. Nigga, it's me.

(*The four respond in horror at the word.*)

CARA. He must be one of those rappers.

(*Beat.*)

Are you Drizzy Drake?

SAMARIA. I don't feel safe.

RICHARD. I feel threatened.

DARRYL. I have a gun over there in that drawer and I've taken lessons on how to use it.

SAMARIA. Don't tell him where your gun is.

CARA. I'm sure he came here with his own.

>   *(Beat.)*

Didn't you, Drizzy Drake?

SIMON. Why y'all trippin'? You two was just talking about Wakanda forever.

>   *(**DARRYL** rushes over to the gun's hiding place. He pulls it out and aims it at **SIMON**.)*

DARRYL. I'm standing my ground. You're all my witnesses. I'm standing my ground.

ALL BUT SIMON. You're standing your ground.

SIMON. Man, have you lost your mind? It's me, your Boi. It's Simon. Where's my mask? Just give me a mask.

>   *(**SIMON** frantically searches the box for his mask.)*

CARA. I think he's looking for a knife. Kill him. Kill him before he kills us. Kill him.

SIMON. Y'all completely caught up in this white bullshit. Just find me a mask.

SAMARIA. Shoot him.

RICHARD. Shoot him, Darryl.

CARA. Shoot Drizzy Drake, Darryl.

CARA, SAMARIA & RICHARD. Shoot him. Shoot him. Shoot him. Shoot him. Shoot him. Shoot him.

>   *(**DARRYL** fires his gun seven times. **SIMON** drops to the floor.)*

DARRYL. I had no choice.

CARA, SAMARIA & RICHARD. You had no choice.

DARRYL. I warned him.

CARA, SAMARIA & RICHARD. You warned him.

DARRYL. You heard me.

CARA, SAMARIA & RICHARD. We heard you. You had no choice. You warned him.

SAMARIA. It was the hoodie.

> (**RICHARD** *lifts his mask and returns to his Blackness. Not liking the reality of seeing his dead friend, he quickly lowers his mask and returns to Caucasian.*)

RICHARD. He had a gun.

CARA. He was being aggressive.

DARRYL. They always get away.

ALL. We had no choice.

> *(Blackout.)*

End of Play

Crush

Krista Knight

CRUSH was first produced by Allyson Morgan, F*It Club at IRT Theater in New York City in 2016. The performance was directed by Matt Dickson, with set and prop design by Polina Minchuk, costume design by Christina Wells Madison, sound design by Daniel Melnick, and light design by Cody Richardson. The production stage manager was Joey Mulica. The cast was as follows:

COCKROACH ....Ben Beckley

CRUSH was subsequently produced by Krista Knight and Barry Brinegar at No Puppet Co. and released on YouTube in 2020. It was directed, designed, and animated by Krista Knight and Barry Brinegar. The cast was as follows:

COCKROACH ....Ben Beckley

CHARACTERS

COCKROACH – A cross between Patrick Bateman and a beatnik poet. Could be wearing a beret. Ideally is on a mic to start. Perhaps becomes more cockroach-like over the course of the play (antennae, etc.).

SETTING

A dilapidated apartment

Scene One

COCKROACH. Crush.

Candy Crush. Crushed ice to make a snow cone.

My blood...the syrup?

You pack it into a little white paper cone – part of a set your girlfriend got you at like a whimsical Restoration Hardware saying, "I can't give this to you on your birthday because you have a weird thing about your birthday so that's why you get this novelty-snow-cone machine now." It's so novel I can't stand it!

Blueberry snow cones and fizzing your own seltzer are just some of the many wonderful summer activities you do when the city gets hot.

Bathing suit.

FLIP!

FLOPS!

You are going to the beach. This is our first summer together. You moved in a month ago.

The last tenant she – why even – you're here now. And your rhythms of stomping are better than any other rhythms. The kind of crumbs you leave and you leave crumbs. Nasty (crumb)...

Flip flop flip flop you're done with your cone.

Flip flop flip flop how many days will you be gone?

Flip flop flip flop flip flop take me flop with flip you.

Scene Two

(Blue smeared on face.)

COCKROACH. Starving.

I haven't eaten for weeks. Without your footfalls the idiots come.

I hate nothing so much as I hate another cockroach.

When will you get tired of the Hamptons and pretending you're rich because I know you're not I live in your walls. The house of the house of the fiancé of the friend of the friend's dad is not your house. Our house. This house. Left with just your blueberry stain. Never has the warmest color felt so cold. Snow cone! Ice of my heart. The paper hasn't tasted sweet for days.

*(***COCKROACH*** licks the paper cone.)*

Scene Three

(Blue gone.)

COCKROACH. Back. You're back. But you seem different. Tan. You're more tan. Weren't you using sun lotion?

Some mail came for you while you were gone. At the beach. Having fun. I chewed through the plastic bubble wrap inner coating to find an expired advent calendar with Christmas crossed out and with a countdown to your birthday. Is your birthday coming up – is that what this is about? What would help? If I complimented you? You don't look ugly. You don't look old.

If you could see yourself right now.

The way I see you.

So incredibly tall and wide your feet create a wind tunnel.

Kind. Messy. Clumsy. Crumsy. You.

Do I only want you because you scare me…

Scene Four

COCKROACH. Stupid. You. Stupid you you little – crumb. My little crumb.

You came a little close to actually just about really stepping on me. You. Better. CUT THAT OUT!

Remember that my exoskeleton is a mere millimeter and I'm hardy it's true but mortal! I have an excellent sense for self-preservation except when I –

I I hear your heels come stomping I can't help but (cum) running.

I'd never hurt *you*. I'd never sleep in your flour. I'd never shit on your bed.

I'd never run over your mouth while you're sleeping.

(Sly smile – he would and has.)

Here's what I'll do – I'll be loose about it. I'll let this one go. You have things on your mind. Events approaching. Encroaching. I'll do something nice for you. I'll make you happy. Would you like that? I'll make you happy...

Scene Five

(Joyous exuberant "naked birthday dance.")

COCKROACH. Birthday it's your birthday birthday it's your birthday birthday it's your birthday

birthday it's your birthday birthday it's your birthday birthday it's your birthday

birthday it's your birthday birthday it's your birthday birthday it's your birthday –

(Ends with a load thud and COCKROACH *scream.)*

Scene Six

*(COCKROACH is an angel cockroach now,
floating above. Heaven music.*)*

COCKROACH. Bare. The bare foot. I bared it all.

And you –

I heard you get up early in the morning. I thought.
Here you come! To the kitchen! For seltzer for snow
cones for me.

But you woke up early to set up for a party. Streamers
and twinkle lights and dip. (I thought you hated your
birthday!)

But you threw a party and filled our apartment with
strangers.

And not all of them took their shoes off.

Bags drop and chairs move and I want to celebrate with
you – we can't get a moment alone together – and it's
almost midnight it's almost over – I run to you to show
you my naked birthday dance. Private. And personal.
And in front of everyone.

And for the first time you really see me. Is that you
scream or me?

Four sets of carbonate wings spread in perfect geometric.
Splatter.

Thorax – splintered.

Waxy calcium carbonate jutting. Through organs.

Eye ocelli compound.

And that's the last I see.

Until I woke here – above *you*.

Now I can watch you always.

Now I can watch you always.

Now I can watch you always.

End of Play